Here Comes Hungry Albert

ABC Adventures

Written by Pat Whitehead

Illustrated by G. Brian Karas

Troll Associates

Library of Congress Cataloging in Publication Data

Whitehead, Patricia.
    Here comes Hungry Albert.

    (ABC adventures)
    Summary: No matter how much he eats, Albert the ape
can always eat more. A letter of the alphabet appears on
each page accompanied by an appropriate word from the
text.
    1. Children's stories, American. [1. Apes—Fiction.
2. Food—Fiction. 3. Alphabet] I. Karas, G. Brian, ill.
II. Title. III. Series.
PZ7.W5852He   1985   [E]   84-8835
ISBN 0-8167-0379-5 (lib. bdg.)
ISBN 0-8167-0380-9 (pbk.)

Copyright © 1985 by Troll Associates, Mahwah, New Jersey.
All rights reserved. No part of this book may be used or
reproduced in any manner whatsoever without written permission
from the publisher.
Printed in the United States of America.

10 9 8 7 6 5 4 3 2 1

Here comes hungry Albert.

Aa

ape

Albert is an ape. He loves to eat.

Bb

bananas

He eats bananas—a bunch at a time.

Cc

carrots

He eats carrots—crunch, crunch.

Dd

doughnuts

He eats doughnuts and milk.

Ee

everything

Albert the ape eats everything.

Ff

full

Are you full, Albert?
Have you had enough?

Gg

growls

Albert growls a big growl.

Hh

hungry

"No, I'm still hungry," he says.

Ii

ice cream

"I want some ice cream."

Jj

just

"Some strawberry ice cream is just what I want."

Kk

know

"And I know where to get some."

HAWTHORNE

Ll

looks

Albert stops and looks both ways.

Mm

marches

Then he marches across the street.

Nn

neighborhood

Hungry Albert walks and walks.
He walks all around the neighborhood.

Oo

over

He climbs over a fence.

Pp

park

He walks straight past the park.

Qq

Quick, quick

Quick, quick—Albert goes faster and faster.

Rr

runs

Albert runs and runs.

Ss

swings

He swings through the trees.

Tt

trots

He trots up the hill.

Uu

Up, up, up

Up, up, up he goes.

Vv

very

He is getting very tired.

Ww

Where

"Whew!" says Albert. "I'm here at last."
Where? Where is Albert?

Xx

"Strawberry, please. With extra sprinkles," says Albert.

Yy

Yum, yum

"Yum, yum."
Do you know where Albert is?

Zz

zoo

not feed the animals!

He's at the zoo.

Albert loves to eat ice cream at the zoo.
"*MMMmmm. Good.*"